LIGHTS OUT!

by Lucille Recht Penner
Illustrated by Jerry Smath

The Kane Press
New York

To Emilia Gertner,.
—L.R.P.

To Roberta Pressel,
—J.S.

Library of Congress Cataloging-in-Publication Data

Penner, Lucille Recht.
   Lights out/by Lucille Recht Penner; illustrated by Jerry Smath.
     p. cm. — (Math matters.)
   Summary: Hoping to be the last person awake, a young girl keeps count as one person after another turns out a light in the apartment building across from hers.
   ISBN 1-57565-092-4 (pbk. : alk. paper)
   [1. Bedtime Fiction. 2. Subtraction Fiction.] I. Smath, Jerry, ill. II. Title. III. Series.
PZ7.P38465Li 2000
[E]—dc21
                                                 99-42678
                                                  CIP
                                                  AC

10 9 8 7 6 5 4 3 2 1

First published in the United States of America in 2000 by The Kane Press.
Printed in Hong Kong.

MATH MATTERS is a registered trademark of The Kane Press.

I'm the youngest kid in my family.
I have to go to sleep before everyone else.
My brother goes to sleep at 10 o'clock.
My sister can stay up until 9:00.
   Guess when I have to go to sleep?
8 o'clock. Is that fair?

Every night is the same. I turn out my light and get into bed. I look out the window.

There is a big apartment building across the street. Almost every light is on—and I have to go to bed.

How can this be fair?

Tonight I count the lights. There are 32 of them. 32!

All those people are still up!

I march into the living room. "I am always the first person in the world to put my light out," I say. "Tonight I want to be the last person to do it. Please let me. There's no school tomorrow."

My mother says, "Okay." My father does too. "You can keep the light on," they tell me. "Just this once."

FANtastic. This will be a great night.

I count the lights again. There were 32
lights before. Now there are only 30. Two
people are already asleep.
Not me!

I write 30 in my notebook. A good start.
I'm going to stay up until every light I see
from my window is out. By then everyone
else in the world will probably be asleep. Ha!

A girl on the first floor
turns out her light.

A minute later 2 lights go
out on the second floor.

Then another. That's 4 lights.

I write 30 minus 4 in my notebook. This is easy. I count back to get the answer. There are 26 lights to go!

I look at my clock. It says 9 o'clock. I've already stayed up one hour longer than I usually do.

And I'm not a bit sleepy.

A woman comes into a room and covers her parrot's cage with a cloth. Then she turns out her light. Is that 2 more? No. I can't count the parrot. It's only 1 light. There are 25 lights left.

In one window I see twin boys. They are having a pillow fight. Their mother comes into the room.

The boys jump into bed. She kisses them and turns out the light. She turns out her light, too. Then 2 more lights go off on the same floor. That's 4 more lights out. 21 still to go!

People sure get sleepy early. I'm a little
sleepy myself. I have an idea to wake myself
up. I'll put on some music and dance.

All of a sudden 6 lights go out! I grab
my notebook. Now I have to regroup to get
the answer. 21 minus 6 is 15!

A man is doing jumping jacks at his
window. It looks like fun. I do a few, too.
The man turns out his light. All the other
lights on his floor go out.

Wow! Do the people on that floor always go to sleep at the same time? There were 8 lights on that floor. 15 minus 8 is 7. Seven lights to go and I will be the last one up. I can hardly wait.

19

Now what? A boy turns out his light, but he starts reading with a flashlight. He reads and reads. That book must be terrific.

"I can't count you if your flashlight is on," I think. "Finish the book tomorrow."

What do you know? The boy turns out the flashlight. 7 minus 1 is 6.

The lights are getting blurry. I must have closed my eyes for a second. I open them very wide and suddenly 3 lights go out. Now only 3 lights are still on.

I'm very sleepy. I doze for a minute. Then my eyes snap open. Great! Only 2 lights are on now. A light must have gone out while I had my eyes closed.

It's hard to be the last one up. But I can do it.

I make funny faces to keep myself awake. I make my dinosaur face. It's awesome! Then I make my laughing hyena face. And I get my reward. A light goes out!

Now there's only 1 light left! Why doesn't it go out? Doesn't that person know how late it is? What's going on over there?

I'm very tired. I close my eyes for just one minute. But I'm not asleep. Definitely not. This is a contest between me and the other person who isn't asleep. And I am going to win. Except I'm so tired. I need to lie down on my bed for...one...second...

When I open my eyes, the sun is shining. It's morning! This is not fair. I wasn't the last one up even though I tried so hard.

I look at the window that had the last light. The shade flies up. There is a boy with a red baseball hat.

I know that boy. He goes to my school. His name is Daniel and he's my age. How could he stay up so late?

Mom and I walk to the playground. I see Daniel coming around the corner. "Boy, you stay up late," I say. "I was up late myself last night. I saw your light."

"Oh," Daniel says, "I always sleep with my light on—because of my little brother. He's such a baby! But the light doesn't bother me. I was asleep by 8:00 last night."

DO NOT
PICK THE
FLOWERS

Yipppeeee! I feel great. This is fairer than fair! I was the last person up last night. I was probably the last person up in the whole world!

But I have to admit I'm really, really tired. I can't wait to go to bed tonight!

SUBTRACTION CHART

Here are some ways to subtract.

1. Count back.   15 − 8 = ?

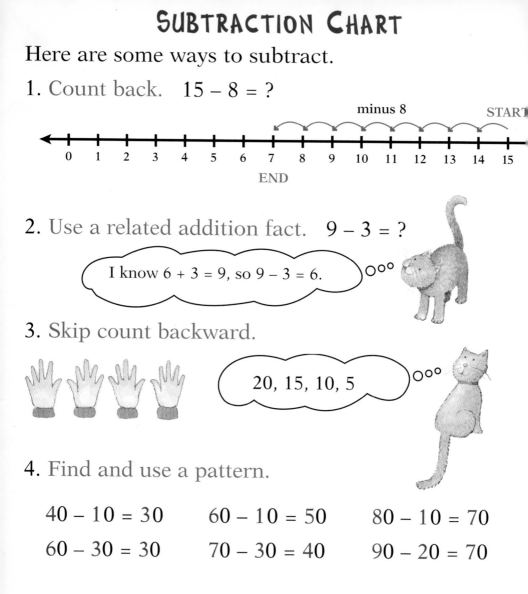

minus 8   START

0 1 2 3 4 5 6 7 8 9 10 11 12 13 14 15

END

2. Use a related addition fact.   9 − 3 = ?

I know 6 + 3 = 9, so 9 − 3 = 6.

3. Skip count backward.

20, 15, 10, 5

4. Find and use a pattern.

40 − 10 = 30   60 − 10 = 50   80 − 10 = 70

60 − 30 = 30   70 − 30 = 40   90 − 20 = 70

5. Use this rule to subtract 2-digit numbers.

First subtract the ones. Then subtract the tens.

		3 11	7 10
54	35	4̸1̸	8̸0̸
− 12	− 4	− 26	− 7
42	31	15	73

No regrouping.   Regroup ones as tens before subtracting.

32